YASMIN

The Detective

written by
SAADIA FARUQI

illustrated by
HATEM ALY

PICTURE WINDOW BOOKS
a capstone imprint

To Mariam for inspiring me, and Mubashir
for helping me find the right words—S.F.

To my sister, Eman, and her amazing girls,
Jana and Kenzi—H.A.

Yasmin is published by Picture Window Books, an imprint of Capstone.
1710 Roe Crest Drive
North Mankato, Minnesota 56003
capstonepub.com

Text copyright © 2023 by Saadia Faruqi.
Illustrations copyright © 2023 by Capstone.

Library of Congress Cataloging-in-Publication Data
Names: Faruqi, Saadia, author. | Aly, Hatem, illustrator.
Title: Yasmin the detective / Saadia Faruqi ; illustrated by Hatem Aly.
Description: North Mankato, Minnesota: Picture Window Books,
[2022] | Series: Yasmin | Audience: Ages 5-8. | Audience: Grades K-1.|
Summary: Nani likes to sit outside and sew, but little things like her
thimble keep disappearing, so Yasmin turns detective and applies a
science lesson to solve the mystery.
Identifiers: LCCN 2021051481 (print) | LCCN 2021051482 (ebook) |
ISBN 9781663959294 (hardcover) | ISBN 9781666331127 (paperback) |
ISBN 9781666331134 (pdf)
Subjects: LCSH: Muslim girls—Juvenile fiction. | Pakistani Americans—
Juvenile fiction. | Crows—Juvenile fiction. | Theft—Juvenile fiction. |
CYAC: Crows—Fiction. | Stealing—Fiction. | Pakistani Americans—
Fiction. | Muslims—United States—Fiction. | LCGFT: Picture books.
Classification: LCC PZ7.1.F373 Ybl 2022 (print) | LCC PZ7.1.F373
(ebook) | DDC [E]—dc23
LC record available at https://lccn.loc.gov/2021051481
LC ebook record available at https://lccn.loc.gov/2021051482

Editorial Credits:
Editor: Kristen Mohn; Designer: Kay Fraser;
Production Specialist: Katy LaVigne

Design Elements:
Shutterstock/LiukasArt

TABLE OF CONTENTS

CHAPTER ONE

Something Missing

It was a beautiful Saturday. The sun was shining. The birds were chirping.

Nani was sewing, and Nana was reading.

Yasmin was helping Baba put up a new bird feeder.

"Done!" said Baba.

Nana looked up. "Birds are very clever," he said. "They can make and use tools."

"And they can recognize people!" Yasmin said. "We're learning about birds in school."

Yasmin realized it was time for her favorite cartoon. It was about an owl named Detective Hoo. He solved mysteries.

Yasmin headed inside. Soon Nani came in too. She looked confused.

"Have you seen my thimble?" she asked.

"I'll help you look," Yasmin said. Detective Hoo was always searching for missing things.

"Where did you last see it?" Yasmin asked.

"It was on the table outside, and then it was gone," Nani replied.

Yasmin went outside. She looked everywhere. On the table. On the chairs. Even in the grass. No thimble. Where could it have gone?

CHAPTER TWO

Detective Work

The next day, birds were fluttering around the new feeder. Some were white. Others were gray. One had a red belly. Yasmin drew them all in her journal.

A big black crow sat on the grass watching her. "Caw, caw!" Yasmin called to it.

After lunch, Nani was puzzled again. "One of the big buttons from my sewing box is missing," she grumbled. "And I can't find my glasses!"

Yasmin had an idea. She got out her journal, just like Detective Hoo.

"Don't worry Nani," she said. "Detective Yasmin is on the case!"

Yasmin interviewed everyone. "Have you seen Nani's missing things?" she asked.

Mama shook her head. "I haven't left the kitchen all morning."

Baba was in the garage. "I'm

sorry, jaan," he said. "I just got

back from the grocery store."

"I've been reading all day,"

Nana said, holding up his book.

This was a real mystery. Where could Nani's missing things be? Yasmin would have to hunt for more clues.

CHAPTER THREE

A Break in the Case

On Monday, Ms. Alex showed the class pictures of birds.

"Some birds collect things," she explained.

Emma raised her hand. "What sorts of things?" she asked.

"Food. Or soft things like lint to make their nests cozy," Ms. Alex replied. "Some birds collect shiny objects."

Yasmin's eyes grew big. Nani's thimble, button, and glasses were all shiny. Yasmin had her first clue!

After school, Yasmin took her journal and binoculars to the backyard. Nani and Baba were sitting on the patio.

"Hello, Yasmin," Baba said.

"Shh," Yasmin said. "I'm doing detective work." She hid behind a bush and watched the birds around the feeder.

Caw! said a crow. Was it the same one from yesterday?

"You're my suspect!" Yasmin

said as she popped out from

behind the bush.

The crow flew to a tree.

Yasmin used her binoculars. She

saw its nest high in the branches.

"Baba!" she said. "I need a ladder, please!"

"A ladder? Why, jaan?" Baba asked.

"I'm about to solve a mystery!" Yasmin said.

Soon, Baba came back down.
He was holding three shiny
objects: a thimble, a button,
and a pair of glasses.

"Nani's things!" Yasmin cried.
"That crow was the thief!"

Nani hugged her. "Shukriya!"
she said. "You solved the
mystery, Detective Yasmin!"

Think About It, Talk About It

* Yasmin uses her detective skills to help her nani. What are some ways you help your family and relatives?

* Yasmin's knowledge about birds helps her solve the case of Nani's missing items. What facts does she learn that make her think the crow might be the suspect?

* Have you ever solved a mystery? What clues did you use to crack the case?

* Make a list of five facts you know about birds (or your favorite animal)!

Learn Urdu with Yasmin!

Yasmin's family speaks both English and Urdu. Urdu is a language from Pakistan. Maybe you already know some Urdu words!

baba (BAH-bah)—father

hijab (HEE-jahb)—scarf covering the hair

jaan (jahn)—life; a sweet nickname for a loved one

kameez (kuh-MEEZ)—long tunic or shirt

kitaab (keh-TAB)—book

lassi (LAH-see)—a yogurt drink

nana (NAH-nah)—grandfather on mother's side

nani (NAH-nee)—grandmother on mother's side

salaam (sah-LAHM)—hello

shukriya (shuh-KREE-yuh)—thank you

Pakistan Fun Facts

Yasmin and her family are proud of their Pakistani culture. Yasmin loves to share facts about Pakistan!

Pakistan is on the continent of Asia, with India on one side and Afghanistan on the other.

Islamabad

PAKISTAN

The word Pakistan means "land of the pure" in Urdu and Persian.

Many languages are spoken in Pakistan, including Urdu, English, Saraiki, Punjabi, Pashto, Sindhi, and Balochi.

The chukar partridge is the national bird of Pakistan. It lives in dry or desert habitats.

The markhor is often considered the national animal of Pakistan. A markhor is a large goat with spiral shaped horns and a fur coat.

Make Binoculars!

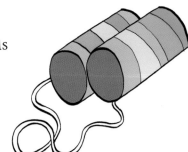

SUPPLIES:

- 2 empty toilet paper rolls
- a single hole punch
- glue
- yarn or string
- markers (optional)

STEPS:

1. Glue together the 2 toilet paper rolls, side by side. Let dry.

2. Ask your parents to help you use the single hole punch to make a hole on one end of each tube, on the outer edge.

3. Thread the yarn or string through the holes and tie knots to secure.

4. Use the markers to decorate your binoculars.

5. Take your binoculars outside and spy on some birds!

Saadia Faruqi is a Pakistani American writer, interfaith activist, and cultural sensitivity trainer featured in *O, The Oprah Magazine*. She also writes middle grade novels, such as *Yusuf Azeem Is Not A Hero*, and other books for children. Saadia is editor-in-chief of *Blue Minaret*, an online magazine of poetry, short stories, and art. Besides writing books, she also loves reading, binge-watching her favorite shows, and taking naps. She lives in Houston, Texas, with her family.

Hatem Aly is an Egyptian-born illustrator whose work has been featured in multiple publications worldwide. He currently lives in beautiful New Brunswick, Canada, with his wife, son, and more pets than people. When he is not dipping cookies in a cup of tea or staring at blank pieces of paper, he is usually drawing books. One of the books he illustrated is *The Inquisitor's Tale* by Adam Gidwitz, which won a Newbery Honor and other awards, despite Hatem's drawings of a farting dragon, a two-headed cat, and stinky cheese.

Join Yasmin on all her adventures!